D0402932

Whooooo Done It?

ANIMAL INN
Whooooo Done It?

Book 5

PAUL DUBOIS JACOBS
&
JENNIFER SWENDER

Illustrated by STEPHANIE LABERIS

ALADDIN

New York   London   Toronto   Sydney   New Delhi

For P-Pop

ALADDIN
An imprint of Simon & Schuster Children's Publishing Division
1230 Avenue of the Americas, New York, New York 10020
First Aladdin hardcover edition May 2018
Text copyright © 2018 by Simon & Schuster, Inc.
Illustrations copyright © 2018 by Stephanie Laberis
Also available in an Aladdin paperback edition.
All rights reserved, including the right of reproduction in whole or in part in any form.
ALADDIN and related logo are registered trademarks of Simon & Schuster, Inc.
For information about special discounts for bulk purchases, please contact
Simon & Schuster Special Sales at 1-866-506-1949 or business@simonandschuster.com.
The Simon & Schuster Speakers Bureau can bring authors to your live event.
For more information or to book an event, contact the Simon & Schuster Speakers Bureau
at 1-866-248-3049 or visit our website at www.simonspeakers.com.
Series designed by Jessica Handelman
Interior designed by Greg Stadnyk
The illustrations for this book were rendered digitally.
The text of this book was set in Bembo Std.
Manufactured in the United States of America 0418 FFG
2 4 6 8 10 9 7 5 3 1
Library of Congress Control Number 2018931974
ISBN 978-1-4814-9963-7 (hc)
ISBN 978-1-4814-9962-0 (pbk)
ISBN 978-1-4814-9964-4 (eBook)

PROLOGUE

Creak! Creak!

Creak! Creak!

This old house sure makes a lot of spooky sounds. There's always something creaking, squeaking, or rattling.

Welcome to Animal Inn. My name is Whiskers. You might also know me as Super Cat, but that's another story.

No, I'm not one of those cats who is always clamoring to get outside. That would be my big sister, Shadow. I am an *indoor* cat. I love calm, quiet, and relaxing on my comfy sofa.

I belong to the Tyler family. Our family includes five humans—Mom, Dad, Jake, Ethan, and Cassie—and seven pets:

- Me
- Shadow—my big sister
- Dash—a Tibetan terrier
- Coco—a chocolate Labrador retriever
- Leopold—a scarlet macaw
- and Fuzzy and Furry—a pair of very enterprising gerbils

We all live together in this creaky old house in the countryside. Animal Inn is one part hotel, one part school, and one part spa. As our brochure says: *We promise to love your pet as much as you do.*

Creak! Creak!

Don't mind that noise. It's just the creaky front door. It gets a lot of use with all the coming and going here at the inn.

We might have a Pekinese arriving for a pedicure. A Siamese showing up for a short stay. Or a llama leaving after a long stay. Once, we even hosted a field trip for Cassie's entire first-grade class. That day was neither calm nor quiet. But it sure was fun.

On the first floor of Animal Inn, we have the Welcome Area, the office, the classroom, the grooming room, and the party and play room.

Our family lives on the second floor. This includes Fuzzy and Furry snug in their gerbiltorium, unless they're out on a job. We Tyler pets have used their detective services on a number of occasions.

The third floor is for our smaller guests. We have a Reptile Room, a Rodent Room, and a Small Mammal Room. The larger guests stay out in the barn and kennels.

That means at any given moment, you might hear squawks, chirps, bleats, meows, or woofs.

And just last week we heard a sound that gave all of us quite a scare.

Promise not to get too frightened?

Okay. Let me tell you what happened. . . .

CHAPTER

1

It all began the first morning of

school vacation week.

We pets were in the Welcome Area.

I was curled up on the sofa.

Leopold was on his perch.

Dash was sitting nearby.

And Coco was plopped smack in the middle of

the floor.

As usual, my big sister, Shadow, was hiding behind the sofa, waiting for her first chance to sneak outside.

Everything was nice and quiet, until Jake and Ethan came charging downstairs.

"I can't wait to play Ghost in the Graveyard," said Ethan.

"But Mom and Dad said chores come first," said Jake. He opened the door to the supply closet. "Let's see. Cat food, cat treats, dog food, dog—hold on. This is strange." Jake held up an empty bag of Doggie Donuts. "I just opened this yesterday."

"Maybe that's a different bag," said Ethan. "And the one you opened is still in there."

Jake searched the closet again. "No, I'm sure this is the bag," he said. "But where did all the treats go?"

"Well, *I* didn't eat them," said Ethan.

"I didn't think you did," said Jake. "But they couldn't have vanished into thin air."

"Let's just open a new bag," said Ethan. "The quicker we feed the pets and tidy up, the quicker we can play Ghost in the Graveyard."

"You're right," said Jake.

The boys went ahead and filled our bowls.

But I noticed that Coco kept right on snoring. She must have been really tired because breakfast is usually Coco's favorite time of day. Along with lunch, snack, and dinner.

Ethan went back to the closet. "Whoa," he said. "What happened to this thing?"

"What happened to what?" asked Jake.

Ethan held up the feather duster—minus most of its feathers.

Just then Cassie came skipping down the stairs.

She held a bright pink feather in her hand.

Jake took one look and chuckled. "I think I see what's going on here," he said. "Cassie, did you borrow a bunch of feathers from the feather duster?"

"Are you and Coco doing an art project or something?" asked Ethan.

I looked over at Coco; she was still sound asleep.

"I'm not doing an art project," said Cassie. "I thought we were playing Ghost in the Graveyard this morning."

"Then what's with the feather?" asked Jake.

"I found it in the hallway upstairs," said Cassie. "It's so soft."

"How did a feather from the Welcome Area feather duster get upstairs?" asked Ethan. "And where are the rest of them?"

"And where are the missing Doggie Donuts?" added Jake.

"I don't know," said Cassie. "Are we going to play Ghost in the Graveyard or not?"

"Maybe a ghost took the feathers and treats," Ethan said with a sly grin.

"There's no such thing as ghosts," said Cassie. "They're just in games and stories and stuff."

"Except . . . ," said Jake.

"Except what?" asked Cassie.

"Haven't you heard about the ghost of Animal Inn?" Jake said. "On dark and windy nights, it scritches and scratches at windows and doors."

"And whatever you do," Ethan continued in a spooky voice, "don't let the ghost inside. Or Animal Inn will be haunted . . . *forever*!"

CHAPTER
2

"Mom! Dad!" Cassie called, running

up the stairs. "Jake and Ethan are trying to scare me."

The boys followed her, giggling and making spooky sounds.

"Boo-o-o-o! Boo-o-o-o!"

I looked over at Dash and Leopold. "The ghost of Animal Inn?" I asked worriedly.

"The boys are just being silly," said Dash.

"There's no such thing as ghosts," said Leopold.

"Never mind about the ghosts, you guys," said Shadow, stepping out from behind the sofa. "I've got *real* problems."

"What kind of problems?" I asked.

"Someone's been taking my stuff," she said. "My favorite piece of yarn and my stash of Kitty Krisps are both missing."

"More missing items?" said Dash.

"Interesting," said Leopold.

"And," Shadow started, "when I find out who's been stealing my—"

"Could you please hold down the chatter?" moaned Coco. She drowsily lifted her head. "I'm trying to sleep."

"Sleep?" scoffed Shadow. "We just woke up."

"And you haven't even touched your breakfast," I said.

"I'm too tired to eat," groaned Coco. "That voice outside kept me up all night."

"A *voice*?" I asked.

"Outside?" said Dash.

"At night?" asked Leopold.

"Yep," said Coco. "It kept asking, *'Who cooks for you? Who cooks for you?'* over and over. It made me so hungry, I had to get a snack."

"So you're the one who took the Doggie Donuts from the supply closet," said Dash.

At least that was one mystery solved.

"No, silly," said Coco. "I can't open the door to the supply closet."

"Then you're the one who took my stash of Kitty Krisps," said Shadow.

"Nope," said Coco. "That wasn't me either."

"You didn't eat a bunch of pink feathers, did you?" I asked.

"Why would I eat feathers?" said Coco. "I had some crackers. Cassie always keeps a few crackers next to her bed."

"Did the voice wake Cassie up too?" asked Leopold.

"No," said Coco. "It was the kind of voice that's easier for a dog to hear than a human. It was low and echoey and . . ."

"*Spooky?*" I said with a shiver.

"How'd you know?" said Coco. "That's a great word for it. *Spooky.*"

CHAPTER 3

Rumble! Rumble!

Rumble! Rumble!

"Now what's *that* noise?" I asked.

"It's probably Coco's tummy," said Shadow.

"No, silly," said Coco. "That noise is coming from upstairs. My tummy is right here. But my tummy is feeling a little empty."

She stood up and lumbered over to her food bowl.

"Shadow does have a point," said Dash. "Coco, maybe the voice you heard last night was just your tummy talking."

"That is a logical explanation," said Leopold. "Coco went to bed hungry, and then she dreamed about a voice asking, *'Who cooks for you? Who cooks for you?'*"

"Nope," said Coco, her mouth full of kibble. "I usually dream about mac-and-cheese and cheese pizza and grilled cheese. I never dream about who's doing the cooking."

"And yet the phrase *'Who cooks for you?'* does sound familiar," said Leopold.

All of a sudden Jake, Ethan, and Cassie came racing down the stairs, screeching.

"Run! Run!" squealed Cassie.

"It's going to get us!" cried Ethan.

"Ghost in the graveyard!" shouted Jake.

Rumble! Rumble!

Rumble! Rumble!

There it was again.

Could there really be a ghost upstairs? I buried my head under a sofa cushion.

I heard footsteps.

"That new bread machine sure can make a racket," said Dad, coming down the stairs.

"It sounds like it's about to launch into space," said Mom.

What a relief! The rumbling was only one of Dad's new gadgets.

I pulled my head out from under the cushion

and resettled myself on my cozy spot.

"It says here," said Dad, reading from a booklet, "the rumbling noise is just the machine mixing up the dough."

"Well," said Mom, "it will be wonderful to have fresh bread when Cousin Jane finally gets here."

"I can't wait to see her," said Dad.

"And I can't wait to meet her new show dog, Precious," said Mom.

Mom opened the door to the office. "Whoa!" She gasped. "What happened in here? There's shredded paper all over the floor."

Dad hurried over. "It looks like someone raided the recycling bin," he said. "Was it the pets?"

"But the door was closed," said Mom. "And the
pets can't open doors."

"And it's not like they can pass through walls,"
said Dad.

But I knew something that could.

And it started with the letter G!

CHAPTER
4

"A ghost?" I whispered.

"As I said earlier," replied Leopold, "there's no such thing as ghosts."

"But what about the paper on the floor?" I asked. "And the missing treats? And the disappearing feathers?"

"And let's not forget about my stolen treasures," huffed Shadow.

"Did you say 'treasures'?" asked Dash. He chuckled. "I think I know what's going on here."

"You do?" I asked.

Dash nodded. "Who collects all sorts of treasures and keeps them in a treasure chest?"

"Pirates?" suggested Coco.

"A treasure chest in *our* attic," said Dash.

It suddenly all made sense to me. "I know!" I said excitedly. "Follow me to the gerbiltorium!"

We rushed upstairs to Jake and Ethan's room.

But Fuzzy and Furry were *not* in their gerbiltorium.

"Don't tell me the gerbils are missing too!" I exclaimed.

"Let's try the attic," said Dash.

He led us up to the third floor, past the Small Mammal Room, past the Reptile Room, and past the Rodent Room. Finally, we came to a set of rickety stairs. We carefully tiptoed up.

I'd never been in the attic before. And no wonder. It was dusty and cobwebby. The whole place gave me the shivers.

The gerbils were frantically pawing through their treasure chest.

"No time to talk," said Fuzzy.

"Please excuse the mess," added Furry.

They tossed things this way and that. A half-eaten Kitty Krisp landed in front of us.

"Aha!" said Shadow. "Where are the rest of them?"

"The rest of what?" asked Fuzzy.

"My Kitty Krisps," said Shadow. "The ones you stole from me."

"We did not steal anything from *you*," said Fuzzy.

"In fact, someone has been stealing from *us*," added Furry.

"Missing item number one," said Fuzzy. "A small silver bell."

"Originally from a fancy cat collar," added Furry.

"That was *my* bell," said Shadow.

"You hated that bell," I reminded her.

"Missing item number two," continued Fuzzy. "One large cashew."

"Partially eaten by me," added Furry.

"And missing item number three," said Fuzzy. "One tiny homemade stuffed animal."

"In the shape of a mouse," added Furry.

"Mousey-Mouse?" Coco asked with concern. "That's Cassie's! She thought she lost it on the school bus."

"She did not lose it on the school bus," said Fuzzy.

"But it is lost now," added Furry.

"Hold your horses, gerbils," said Shadow. "Things don't just vanish into thin air. If you two aren't taking the stuff, then who is?"

I felt the fur on the back of my neck rise.

"Could it be the ghost of Animal Inn?" I asked.

"A ghost?" said Fuzzy. "Leave it to us, then!"

"We are expert ghost hunters," added Furry.

They quickly piled everything back into their treasure chest and disappeared into the heating vent.

CHAPTER
5

With Fuzzy and Furry on the

case, the rest of us headed back downstairs to the
Welcome Area.

I curled up on the sofa. Shadow hid behind it.
Leopold flew to his perch. Dash sat nearby. And
Coco plopped down smack in the middle of the
floor.

Everything was calm and quiet.

Ding-dong!

"At last," said Shadow, "a chance to sneak outside."

"Please don't go outside today," I pleaded. "There might be a ghost out there."

"I'll be fine, Little Brother," she said.

Ding-dong!

Mom and Dad hurried out of the office to answer the front door.

"Jane!" said Mom. "So great to see you!"

Cousin Jane gave Mom and Dad a big hug.

"Sorry I'm a little late," said Cousin Jane. "It always takes longer to get out of the house than I think it will."

"Jake! Ethan! Cassie!" Dad called. "Cousin Jane is here!"

The kids rushed in from the party and play room.

"And this must be Precious," said Mom. She gestured to the strangest-looking creature I had ever set eyes on. It was big and white and . . . How should I say this?

Moppy.

"What kind of dog is she?" Ethan asked.

Wait. This thing was a *dog*?

"She's a commander dog," said Cassie.

"Close," Mom said with a smile, "she's a komondor."

"Komondors are working dogs," added Cousin Jane. "Well, not Precious. Precious is a show dog. But her ancestors were prized guard dogs."

"She's really cool-looking," said Jake.

"Supercool," said Ethan.

"Her coat naturally forms these thick cords," explained Cousin Jane. "They help to protect the dog and also let her blend in with a flock of sheep."

"I think she's magical," said Cassie. "She can play princesses with me and Coco."

Coco excitedly bounded over to say hello.

Grrrr! Precious growled.

"Now, Precious . . . ," said Cousin Jane.

"It's okay," said Mom. "Coco can come on a little strong."

Dash calmly wagged his tail and approached our new guest.

Grrrr! Precious growled again.

"Precious," said Cousin Jane, "you mustn't get yourself too worked up."

"Why don't I take Coco and Dash with me out to the barn and kennels?" said Dad. "I have to check on the guests anyway. We'll let Precious get settled in."

Wait. Shouldn't Precious be the one heading out to the kennels?

Dad took down the leashes. Then he led Dash and Coco carefully around Precious and out the front door.

"Can Precious play with us?" asked Cassie.

"What are you playing?" asked Cousin Jane.

"Ghost in the Graveyard," said Ethan.

"Sounds scary," said Cousin Jane.

"Not really," said Jake. "It's like hide-and-seek."

"Well, Precious doesn't play a lot of games," said Cousin Jane. "She's usually busy training for a show. Practice make perfect, you know."

"Maybe you can all play a little later," said Mom. "First you boys have a habitat to tidy up."

"Which habitat?" asked Jake. "We already did our chores."

"*Your* habitat," Mom said with a smile. "Cousin Jane will be staying in Cassie's room, which means Cassie will be in your room in her sleeping bag."

"Yay! Camping!" cheered Cassie.

"Now, I don't want you kids making a lot of noise all night," said Mom. "Cousin Jane has a big day tomorrow."

"No worries," said Cousin Jane. "I sleep like a rock."

"Well, let's show you to your room," said Mom.

She and Cousin Jane started up the stairs. The kids followed.

"Aren't you coming, Precious?" asked Cousin Jane.

But Precious had a different plan.

She hopped up onto the sofa and stretched her paws over the edge. Then she crossed them elegantly.

"Suit yourself," said Cousin Jane. "I'll be right back."

Now I know it's not *my* sofa, but Precious sure took up a lot of it.

This day was quickly going from bad to worse. On top of the missing treasures and the spooky voice and the mysterious mess in the office, I now had to share the sofa?

Precious sniffed at the air and made a sour face. "I'm bored," she said.

CHAPTER 6

At Animal Inn we do promise to love your pet as much as you do. But I was starting to wonder if this fancy show dog was going to put our motto to the test.

Precious let out a long sigh. "What kind of accommodations do you have here, anyway?"

"For which guests?" Leopold asked from his perch. "The third floor is for smaller animals. We have a Reptile Room, a Rodent Room, and a—"

"Reptiles and rodents!" exclaimed Precious. "I will *not* stay near any reptiles or rodents."

"Oh, don't worry," I assured her. "Dog guests stay out in the kennels."

"The *kennels*?" Precious said in disbelief. "I don't stay in kennels. I am competing in a very important show tomorrow. Jane probably booked me into the luxury suite."

"The what?" I asked.

"It's a special room," explained Leopold.

"Oh," I said. "Like the giant lizard habitat in the basement?"

"Lizard? Basement?" Precious snorted. "I don't think so."

"Our last guest to stay there, Miss KD, found it quite delightful," said Leopold.

"Let's change the subject," said Precious. "What about the menu? Who cooks for you?"

"What did you just say?" I asked.

"Who cooks for you?" Precious repeated. "Who's your chef?"

"Uh, Mom and Dad," I said.

"And what kinds of treats do you offer?" asked Precious.

"Kitty Krisps," I said. "I mean, those are for the cats. We have Doggie Donuts for the dogs."

"Doggie Donuts are so *blah*," scoffed Precious. "Luckily, I travel with a supply of my favorite treats, Poochie Puffs." She sprang off the sofa and strutted over to one of Cousin Jane's bags. She grabbed the bottom of the bag in her mouth and flipped it upside down.

Everything spilled out. What a mess! There were

dog toys and dog booties, a dog jacket and a dog brush, an extra dog collar. But no dog treats.

"I know we packed them," Precious said, pawing through the items on the floor. "They couldn't have just vanished into thin air."

Oh no. Had something else mysteriously disappeared?

"Not a problem," said Precious. "I know how to get what I want."

She started to whine . . . softly at first. Then louder. And LOUDER. What a noise!

Cousin Jane came rushing down the stairs. She stopped short when she saw the overturned bag and all the supplies strewn about.

I was sure Precious was about to get scolded, but I was wrong.

"Precious, sweetie," said Cousin Jane, "you

mustn't get yourself too worked up. Would you like a Poochie Puff?" She reached into her pocket and pulled out a small bag of treats. And just like that, Precious stopped whining.

Cousin Jane gave a few treats to Precious, who immediately turned around and jumped back onto the sofa. Then Cousin Jane cleaned up the mess on the floor.

"Let's try to stay calm and quiet," Cousin Jane cooed. "Just like your little cat friend here."

She patted Precious on the top of her head. Then Cousin Jane headed back upstairs, taking the bag of doggie supplies with her.

"That was an impressive display," Leopold said to Precious.

"Oh, you haven't seen anything yet," she replied. "I am a dog of many talents."

CHAPTER
7

Precious began telling Leopold
and me all about her shows and travels.

"Once, Jane and I stayed in a real castle," she
said. "I even met a princess."

"Cassie would have loved that," I said.

"Another time," Precious continued, "we sailed
on a cruise ship to a dog show on a tropical island."

"That sounds delightful," said Leopold.

"It was okay," said Precious. "But I wasn't allowed to play in the ocean. And I was really hot!"

Thump! Thump!

Precious sat up and growled. "What's that noise?" she asked.

"It's probably just Dad's bread machine again," I said. "It makes a racket."

"But that noise isn't coming from upstairs," Leopold pointed out.

He was right. This noise was coming from . . . the window?

Thump! Thump! THUMP! THUMP!

It was Shadow! My big sister was perched outside the window, frantically thumping on the glass with her paws. Her fur was all puffed up in alarm.

"That kitty looks a fright," said Precious. "She could use a good grooming."

"This is a first," said Leopold. "Shadow seems to be trying to get *inside* instead of out."

I leaped off the sofa. "We need to let her in!" I cried. I frantically pawed at the front door. But it was shut tight. "We have to open this door," I pleaded.

"Relax, my little cat friend," said Precious. "As I told you, I am a dog of many talents."

Precious got down off the sofa and stretched her legs. Then she strode over to the door. She placed her front paws on the knob and, balancing on her back legs, nimbly turned it. The front door sprang open.

Shadow zoomed inside. "Shut it, quick!" she cried. She was trembling.

Precious nudged the door closed with her nose.

"What happened to *you*?" I asked Shadow. Usually, it was *me* doing the trembling.

"I . . . I . . . I . . . ," Shadow started. She could barely catch her breath.

"My goodness," said Leopold. "You look like you've seen a—"

"Ghost?" I gulped.

Shadow nodded and darted behind the sofa.

I looked over to Leopold. "I thought you said there was no such thing as ghosts."

"There must be a logical explanation," said Leopold. "I can't believe Shadow saw a real ghost."

"I saw what I saw," said Shadow, peeking out from behind the sofa. "It was a phantom, silently swooping through the sky."

"I'm finding this all very exciting," said Precious.

"I'm certainly not bored anymore. Is this like a show? Did you put it together just for me?"

"*Who* is this?" asked Shadow.

"This is Precious," I said. "Cousin Jane's dog."

"She's the one who opened the door for you," added Leopold.

"No kidding," said Shadow. "You need to teach me how to do that sometime."

"It would be my pleasure," said Precious. "It always works."

To prove her point, Precious walked over to the basement door. Once again, she balanced on her back legs, placed her front paws on the knob, and turned it. The door popped open.

"Very cool," said Shadow.

Just then Fuzzy and Furry tumbled out of the heating vent, one after the other.

"Oh, goodie!" cheered Precious. "Acrobats!"

"There's a ghost outside!" cried Fuzzy.

"Swooping through the sky!" added Furry.

"As usual," said Shadow, "you clowns are a little late."

"Oh, they're clowns?" said Precious. "Even better."

"Batten down the hatches!" cried Fuzzy.

"Lock the doors!" added Furry.

"Yay!" cheered Precious. "A show with audience participation!"

She dashed back over to the front door and pressed the button on the knob to lock it.

"I'm having so much fun," she said, scampering to the sofa. "Jane never lets me play with other pets."

Scritch! Scratch!

Rattle! Rattle!

We all froze. This noise was not coming from
upstairs.

Scritch! Scratch!

Rattle! Rattle!

And it was not coming from the window.

Something was at the front door.

"Don't let it get inside!" screeched Fuzzy.

"Or Animal Inn will be haunted forever!" cried Furry.

I buried my head under a sofa cushion.

Leopold shielded himself with one wing.

Fuzzy and Furry disappeared back into the heating vent.

Shadow darted behind the sofa.

But Precious remained happily where she was. "This is an amazing show," she said. "Such suspense."

CHAPTER
9

Just then Mom and Cousin Jane

came down the stairs.

"I told you Precious would be fine," said Mom.

"You were right," said Cousin Jane. "Everything here seems calm and quiet."

Calm and quiet? *Scared stiff* was more like it.

Scritch! Scratch!

Rattle! Rattle!

There it was again.

"It sounds like someone's at the door," said Cousin Jane.

"That's funny," said Mom. "I didn't hear the bell."

I couldn't look. I squeezed my eyes tight. I could hear Mom's footsteps crossing the Welcome Area.

Then I heard the front door swing open.

"Who locked the door?" asked a familiar voice.

Dad?

"I guess it got locked by mistake," said Mom.

I peeked out from behind my sofa cushion. Dad stood in the doorway with Dash and Coco still on their leashes.

"Can the dogs stay out just a little longer?" asked Mom. "Martha should be here any minute. Then Precious will be in the grooming room for quite a while."

"A while?" asked Dad.

"It takes an hour to wash her and several hours for her to dry," explained Cousin Jane. "Then we have to put on her special grooming jacket to keep her clean until showtime."

"Got it," said Dad. "See you in a bit." He turned to lead Dash and Coco back outside.

Precious inched closer to me. "I don't want to miss any of the fun, little cat friend," she whispered. "Watch this."

Precious started to whine just like before . . . softly at first. Then louder. And LOUDER.

What a noise!

Cousin Jane hurried over. "Precious, sweetie, you mustn't get yourself too worked up."

Cousin Jane reached into her pocket and pulled out the small bag of treats. "Do you want more

Poochie Puffs?" She placed some on the sofa in front of Precious.

But Precious just turned her head and kept right on fussing.

"Or do you want Squishy Squirrelly?" Cousin

Jane asked hopefully. She rifled through the bag on her shoulder. "Now, that's strange."

"What is it?" asked Mom.

"I know I packed her little rubber squirrel," said Cousin Jane. "Maybe I left it upstairs."

Or maybe this was one more thing that had vanished into thin air.

Ding-dong!

"That should be Martha," said Mom.

Luckily, it was.

"Hi, all!" said Martha, stepping inside.

Mom introduced Martha to Cousin Jane.

"And this must be Precious," gushed Martha. "Wow, you're beautiful!"

Precious paused her whining long enough to listen to Martha's compliments.

"I see you've got some Poochie Puffs there," Martha said. She picked a treat up and held it out to Precious. "Why don't we enjoy this in the grooming room?"

Precious stretched and stepped down off the sofa.

"That's a good girl," said Martha.

She led Precious back to the grooming room. Mom and Cousin Jane followed close behind.

CHAPTER
10

Dash, Coco, and Dad soon returned.

Dad unclipped the leashes and hung them by the door.

Then he pulled the instruction booklet out of his back pocket. "I should go check on my bread," he said, heading upstairs. "It says here, the bread should be almost done."

"Are you two okay?" I asked Dash and Coco fretfully.

"Now that you mention it," said Coco, "I am a little hungry. Hey, are those Poochie Puffs?" She gobbled up the treats that Precious had left behind.

"Never mind about your fancy dog snacks," snapped Shadow, popping out from behind the sofa. "We've got bigger fish to fry."

"No, thank you," said Coco. "I'm not in the mood for fish."

"I don't mean real fish," said Shadow. "I mean, what's our plan for dealing with the ghost out there?"

"I thought we agreed earlier that there's no such thing as ghosts," said Dash.

"*Well* . . . ," said Leopold. "There have been some developments."

"I saw it with my own eyes," insisted Shadow. "A phantom, swooping through the sky."

"And we saw it too!" said Fuzzy and Furry, tumbling out of the heating vent.

"It was just like Shadow described," said Fuzzy.

"A spooky, swooping phantom!" added Furry.

"There must be a logical explanation," said Dash. "Maybe it was a crow."

"It was not a crow," said Fuzzy. "We were *with* the crows!"

"In the crow's nest," added Furry.

"Maybe it was a kite," suggested Coco.

"Nobody's flying a kite today," huffed Shadow. "The kids are playing . . . What are they playing, again?"

"Uh, Ghost in the Graveyard," I muttered.

"Not helpful," said Shadow.

"Maybe it was an airplane," said Dash. "Or a helicopter."

"But it made no noise," said Fuzzy.

"It was as silent as the wind," added Furry.

Dash thought for a moment. "Maybe it was a—"

"Ghost!" shouted Cassie.

"Ghost in the graveyard!" Ethan shrieked with laughter.

Cassie and Ethan came racing down the stairs.

Jake chased after them. "And it's going to get you!"

CHAPTER
11

That night, I snuggled close to
Shadow on the big rocking chair in Mom and
Dad's room. It's my favorite place upstairs, especially when Mom leaves a cuddly blanket on the
seat for us to curl up in.

The rest of the day had been uneventful. Precious
had gotten used to Dash and Coco. There had
been no more strange noises. There had been no

more mysterious disappearances of treats, toys, or feathers.

Animal Inn was calm and quiet.

I could finally get some sleep.

Ah-o-o-o-o-o-o-oh!

My eyes shot open.

What was that?

The sound was like a spooky howl. Was it coming from *inside* the house?

Ah-o-o-o-o-o-o-oh!

Shadow stood bolt upright.

"Did you hear that, Little Brother?" she whispered.

"Y-y-yes," I said, trembling.

Ah-o-o-o-o-o-o-oh!

This time the sound woke up Mom.

"Did you hear that?" she whispered to Dad.

"Hear what?" he asked sleepily.

Ah-o-o-o-o-o-o-oh!

"There it is again," said Mom.

"It sounds like it's coming from the Welcome Area," said Dad.

The Welcome Area? It really was inside the house!

Mom and Dad climbed out of bed. Shadow and I cautiously followed them down the stairs.

In the Welcome Area, an eerie apparition hovered near the window. It was tall and billowing and a ghostly shade of white.

Ah-o-o-o-o-o-o-oh!

I darted behind my big sister.

Dad turned on the light.

"Precious?" said Mom sleepily.

Precious had her front paws up on the windowsill.

She was still wearing her special white grooming jacket.

"What are you doing down here, sweetie?" asked Mom. "You should be in Cassie's room with Cousin Jane."

"She probably heard something go bump in the night," said Dad. "This old house does make a lot of strange noises."

"Come up to bed, Precious," said Mom. "You've got a big day tomorrow."

But Precious jumped up onto the sofa and stretched out.

"Okay, you can stay down here," said Mom. "As long as you get some sleep."

Dad turned off the light. Then Mom and Dad headed back up the stairs. Shadow and I did too.

"Pssst," Precious whispered. "Little cat friends. Wait."

We stopped and turned around.

"Your dad was right," she whispered. "I did hear something. But it wasn't a bump in the night. It was a voice."

"A voice?" I asked.

"Yes," said Precious. "It was low and echoey and . . ."

"Spooky?" I offered.

"Exactly," said Precious.

"What did this voice say?" asked Shadow.

"It kept saying, *'Loose hooks and glue. Loose hooks and glue.'* Over and over again," said Precious.

"*'Loose hooks and glue'*?" said Shadow. "That doesn't make any sense."

"Well, maybe it wasn't that," said Precious.

"Maybe it was, *'Goose books in stew. Goose books in stew.'*"

Shadow rolled her eyes. "That makes even *less* sense."

"Or *'Two boots a shoe? Two boots a shoe?'*" tried Precious.

"Hold on," I said. "Any chance the voice was saying, *'Who cooks for you? Who cooks for you?'*"

"Yes! That's it!" said Precious.

"Coco heard that same voice last night," I said.

"And I thought it was just her tummy talking," said Shadow.

"Well, we should be safe now," said Precious. "I think I scared it away with all my howling. My ancestors were prized guard dogs, you know."

"Maybe we should all stick together tonight," I suggested.

"There is safety in numbers," said Shadow.

Shadow and I jumped up onto the sofa and snuggled close to Precious.

Precious sighed happily. "This is like a slumber party," she said. "Jane never lets me have slumber parties."

Everything was again calm and quiet.

I reminded myself that ghosts were only in stories and games. I could finally get some sleep.

CHAPTER
12

Except I couldn't sleep. I thought

I heard something.

Skitter. Skitter.

Patter. Patter.

I looked over at Shadow, but she was snoring softly. She was probably exhausted from her ghostly encounter outside earlier in the day.

Precious was also sound asleep, and I didn't

want to wake her. She had a big show tomorrow.

This sound was probably nothing to worry about. Like Dad had said, this old house can make a lot of strange noises. It was just something going bump in the night.

Bump!

Skitter. Skitter.

Wait. There it was again. It was faint. I listened carefully.

Then I heard a tiny voice whisper, "I'm sure that door is here somewhere."

"Shhh," hushed another voice. "We don't want to wake them."

I blinked my eyes to adjust them to the darkness.

I could see two little figures along the baseboard. They dragged tiny overstuffed sacks behind them.

Was it Fuzzy and Furry? What were they doing up at this hour?

"Hey, guys," I whispered. "Wait."

But they had already disappeared down into the basement.

I quietly slipped off the sofa. Luckily, the basement door was still open a crack. I nudged it with my nose.

Halfway down the stairs a cobweb brushed against my whiskers. I froze in my tracks. The basement felt even scarier than the attic.

"This must be it," whispered the first voice.

That didn't sound like Fuzzy.

"Are you sure it's safe to stay here?" asked the other voice.

And that was definitely *not* Furry.

"The gerbils said we could make ourselves at home in the Komodo dragon habitat."

"Dragon?" said a third, even tinier voice.

"It's just the name of a lizard. It hasn't lived here in months," said the first voice.

Now I could see. It wasn't Fuzzy and Furry at all. It was a family of mice.

They dragged their sacks to the far corner, leaving a trail of dropped items across the floor. I spotted a Kitty Krisp, some bits of shredded paper, and a pink feather.

The littlest mouse clung tightly to a stuffed animal in the shape of . . . Mousey-Mouse?

Aha!

Our things hadn't disappeared. They'd been taken by a family of field mice!

The littlest mouse hugged Mousey-Mouse

even tighter. "I'm still scared," she squeaked.

"It will be safer indoors," said the father mouse.

"We're out of the meadow," said the mother mouse, "and away from that phantom in the sky."

A phantom?

In the sky?

I raced back up the stairs.

It was time to wake Shadow and Precious.

CHAPTER
13

But the phantom beat me to it.

The moment I reached the Welcome Area, a dark shadow swooped past the window.

Then it let out its eerie cry: *"Who cooks for you? Who cooks for you?"*

Shadow and Precious sprang upright.

"That's the voice I was telling you about!" said Precious. "Don't worry. I'm on it." She leaped off the sofa and hurried over to the window.

Ah-o-o-o— she started to howl.

"Wait, Precious," I said quickly. "You'll wake up Mom and Dad. And this time they'll bring you back upstairs."

"I wouldn't want that," said Precious. "I need to stay here and protect you."

Creak! Creak!

I looked over to the stairs. Was it Mom and Dad already? No, it was only Dash and Leopold cautiously making their way down.

"What a relief. It's only you guys," said Dash.

"You gave us quite a fright," added Leopold.

Creak! Creak!

This time it was a sleepy Coco.

"That voice woke me up again," she moaned. "And now I'm hungry." Coco sniffed around the

floor a bit. "Oh, look," she said, "a Doggie Donut! And here's a piece of yarn."

"That's mine!" said Shadow.

"And here's a pink feather," said Dash. "Where did these things come from?"

"I think I can explain," I said.

I told everyone about the family of field mice that had just moved into the basement.

"From the looks of it, they had their whole house on their backs," I added.

"And a few things from our house too," huffed Shadow.

"I'm sure they didn't mean any harm," said Coco.

"Well, I still want my treasures back," said Shadow. "Where are those rodents now?"

Fuzzy and Furry popped out of the heating vent.

"You called?" they asked.

"Not you two!" said Shadow. "The *other* rodents. The mice who took our stuff."

"You mean our clients?" said Fuzzy. "We're helping them find a new home."

"We're expert house hunters," added Furry.

"But the basement is so gloomy," I said.

"Oh, the basement is only temporary," said Fuzzy.

"Until we can find them more suitable accommodations," added Furry.

"But why would they leave their old home?" asked Coco.

As if on cue, the ghostly shadow swooped past the window.

"Who cooks for you? Who cooks for you?"

CHAPTER
14

"It's the ghost of Animal Inn!"

I cried.

"Don't get yourself too worked up," said Precious.

"It's time we solved this mystery once and for all."

"How?" I asked.

"By going outside," she said.

"But I'm an indoor cat," I said.

"I'm with you, Little Brother," said Shadow.

"Last time I went outside, I couldn't wait to get back *inside*."

"And I'm too hungry to go outside," said Coco, plopping down onto the floor.

"We can't go anyway," said Dash. "The front door is shut for the night."

"Oh, that's not a problem," said Precious.

She hurried over to the door. And just like before, she placed her front paws on the knob and nimbly turned it.

Click. The door sprang open.

"Wow," said Dash.

"Precious is a dog of many talents," said Leopold.

"C'mon, everybody!" said Precious. "This is so exciting!"

And without missing a beat, she marched right out into the night.

"Precious!" I called after her. I couldn't let her go alone.

It took all my courage, but I jumped off the sofa and scampered after my new friend.

"Whiskers!" Shadow called. She ran to catch up with me.

I turned to see Dash and Coco rounding out our group, with Leopold perched on Dash's back.

The night was eerily silent.

Step by careful step, we crept along the front walk. Precious led the way, bravely shielding her Animal Inn flock.

Then we heard it again.

"Who cooks for you? Who cooks for you?"

The voice was even louder and scarier.

I looked up. A shadow swooped overhead.

"Can we go back inside now?" I whispered.

"Yeah," said Shadow. "This is really creeping me out."

"Probably a wise idea," said Dash.

"Agreed," said Leopold.

"And I'm still hungry," said Coco.

"Fiddlesticks," said Precious. "Jane never lets me play outside after dark."

We quickly turned to head back inside. But before taking even one step, we stopped in our tracks.

A billowy figure loomed above us. A pair of big round eyes glowed brightly in the darkness.

"The ghost of Animal Inn!" I screeched.

But even the ghost seemed startled.

"A ghost?" it asked in alarm. "Where?" Its head spun in almost a complete circle.

"Here," Shadow said. "*You're* the ghost."

"Me? A ghost?" it said. "I think there's been a mistake. I'm not a ghost. I'm Bartholomew."

Bartholomew inched over to a sliver of moonlight.

He was brown and white and covered in feathers. He had a small yellow beak. He stretched his wings wide and then settled them back at his sides.

"I knew that call sounded familiar," said Leopold. "'Who cooks for you?' is the call of the barred owl."

Bartholomew nodded. "And perhaps you could help me," he said. "I was supposed to be at my brother's two days ago, but I seem to be flying in circles. I'm just terrible with directions."

"You mustn't get yourself too worked up," said Precious.

"We'd be happy to help," said Dash.

"Welcome to Animal Inn," I said.

"Thank you," said Bartholomew. "You are all very kind. I'm trying to reach Pine Valley."

"Oh, I know Pine Valley," said Shadow. "I took the school bus there once. It's due north of here. You make a left at the second pond. That's the tricky part."

"Oh, the *second* pond," said Bartholomew. "That's where I've gone wrong. Thank you. Well, I really must be going."

"So soon?" said Precious. "Why don't you stay a little longer? We're having a slumber party."

"I do love slumber parties," said Bartholomew. "Especially since I'm nocturnal. It's fun when everybody else stays up late too. But maybe next time."

Then he spread his wings and flew off into the night.

"Who cooks for you? Who cooks for you?"

"Now *that* was exciting!" said Precious. "Jane never lets me meet barred owls in the middle of the night."

"But we never gave Bartholomew the answer," said Coco.

"What answer?" I asked.

"Mom and Dad, silly," said Coco. "They're the ones who cook for us."

EPILOGUE

I learned a lot of important lessons from our ghostly adventure:

1. Animal Inn makes a surprising number of spooky sounds.

2. Despite what Coco's tummy might tell you, *"Who cooks for you?"* is the call of the barred owl.

3. Ghosts are only in games and stories.

4. Making a new friend is . . . Precious.

The next morning sunlight filled the Welcome Area.

Everything was calm and quiet.

I opened my eyes and stretched.

Leopold was perched on the arm of the sofa, still dozing. Dash, Coco, Precious, and Shadow lay in a sleepy jumble all around me.

"Look how cute," Cassie whispered from the stairs.

"They're all cuddled up together," said Ethan.

"It's a real slumber party," said Jake.

"How did they end up down here?" asked Mom.

"I was sure Precious was with me the whole night," said Cousin Jane.

"Well, not the *whole* night," said Dad.

"Oh, look!" said Cassie. She bent down and picked something up off the floor. "Here's Shadow's bell."

"That's been missing for ages," said Jake.

Cassie gave the bell a little shake. "And it still works. Now we'll always know where she is."

Shadow opened one eye. "Drat," she whispered.

"Precious," Cousin Jane said quietly. "Time to wake up, sweetie. It's show day. And look who I found." She held out a toy. "Can you believe Squishy Squirrelly was in the bag the whole time?"

Precious snuggled close to me. "I'm going to miss you, my little cat friend," she whispered.

"Oh, Precious," I said with a smile. "Don't get yourself too worked up."

After Cousin Jane and Precious packed up and

left. Mom and Dad headed into the office. The kids went to feed the guests on the third floor.

I settled back into my spot on the sofa.

Leopold flew to his perch.

Dash sat nearby.

Shadow scampered behind the sofa, ready to sneak outside.

And Coco plopped down smack in the middle of the floor.

Everything was back to normal. Well, not quite.

I heard Ethan holler from upstairs. "*I* didn't do it!"

"Then who checked them in?" Jake shouted back.

"Wait. Is that Mousey-Mouse in the habitat?" asked Cassie.

"Mom! Dad!" Jake yelled. "Who checked a family of field mice into the Rodent Room?"

"It wasn't me," Mom called from the office.

"Me either," said Dad.

I knew just who it was, and it wasn't a ghost.

But it did start with the letter G.